Tales of the Captain Duke

The Stowaway Debutante

Rebecca Diem

Cover art by Sarah Dier-McComb
Cover design by Krys Huot-Ricketts

First Edition

Published by Rebecca Dier-McComb
ISBN: 978-0-9938874-1-3

To my parents (R&K),
my grandparents (R&M&B&P),
and everyone who took the time to tell me a story.

Table of Contents

Chapter 1: In which our heroine finds herself in an unlikely predicament

It had been quite easy to sneak onto the airship. Easier still to carve out a hiding place between the stacks of crates and the wall. Clara had a rather comfortable berth under the circumstances. The sacks of grain piled here and there in the cargo hold were more than adequate for her journey to London, though she very much hoped it would be a short one. She spent her time considering various plans for her arrival and snacking on the food she had hurriedly packed: a few early apples, a chunk of yellow cheese, two soft buns, and a small cake with summer berries. The apple made a pleasant crunch as she bit into it, staring through a porthole at the passing landscape below. The airborne vessel drifted over the English countryside as she considered her options.

Clara estimated the trip to be no longer than a half day's journey, or so she judged by the speed with which they crossed to the mainland from the airship docks on the Isle of Wight. She hoped she could eventually make a run for it and get lost in the midday bustle of the London docks, but first she needed to return to solid ground. Her brother Archie's glider might have been useful to this purpose, but once he saw her safely below deck he'd had to be off or risk discovery himself. The glider was far too cumbersome to be hidden, and it would likely be of little use to her once she made it to London. She would have to find some other method of escape. Her best bet to avoid discovery was likely to conceal herself in one of these crates. Clara sighed and stood, brushing the dust from her dress. Resolving to find more appropriate attire upon her arrival, she went to examine the nearest crate.

The cover was firmly in place. She looked around the hold for something useful and discovered a crowbar resting by the steps. She was quite pleased with her progress. It would be a simple matter of replacing one of the grain sacks with herself when the time came to unload the ship. She crossed the room to retrieve the tool, gathering the excess material of her skirts at her hip as she climbed out from her hiding place. Crates were stacked three deep around a large open area in the center of the hold. She retrieved the iron bar and placed the slimmer end into the edge of a large crate marked "GRAINS AND ASST. GOODS." Clara pulled with all her strength, bracing her low-heeled boot against a neighbouring case. The *crack* that followed was louder than she anticipated, but she was certain that the noise of the propellers and engine would mask it. What she had not expected were the contents of the crate.

Gunpowder.

Clara had just begun to ponder this new problem as she recovered from the shock, when footsteps coming down the stairs sent her scrambling to hide as silently as she could. She clutched the crowbar tightly as her veins filled with ice.

"I swear, I heard something," the first voice called out. The sound of three pairs of heavy boots carried through the hold.

"Maybe one of the boxes fell?" suggested a more timid voice.

"If it did it'll be you taking a flight over the rail, boy. The Captain said it was to be handled with *care*. With care! Heard of it?" a loud voice boomed, and the sound of a brief scuffle followed. Behind the crates, Clara held her breath, straining to make sense of their movements and position through sound alone. She had a sinking feeling that this was no simple merchant's ship, and the barely restrained violence of the loud man's voice did not lend itself to a diplomatic resolution if she were caught.

"Leave him be, Johnny, the kid is alright. Nothing seems out of place," the first voice spoke again.

"Well check and be sure, I won't have the Captain taking his displeasure out of our pay, or I'll take my share out of the boy."

Clara stole a quiet breath of relief when the loud man's boots retreated toward the stairwell. She could hear the other two moving about the hold, and hoped that her own thudding heartbeat would not betray her position. She quickly thought through her options: Could she bribe them? Should she fight? Could she run? She made herself as small as possible and waited, every instinct on high alert. The lighter pair of footsteps was getting closer.

A shuffle. A step. He must be less than four feet from her, only the crate she huddled against blocking her from his view. When his voice called out the blood froze in Clara's veins.

"Hey, look over here!"

"What do you got?"

"It's… an apple core, I think."

Damn! She cursed herself for not paying better attention to her waste. To come all this way and fail for leaving an apple core on top of the stacks, she might as well have posted a sign.

"You been snacking on the job?"

"No, I swear. It's not mine."

"Mine neither. Take a look around the stacks over there. Maybe there's more."

This was it. She would be discovered and arrested, maybe killed, or worse, taken back to the Isle in shame. Clara was about to give herself up to their mercy, when shouts came from the decks above.

"What's that?" the first speaker called out.

A series of heavy thuds answered him.

"Hell, it's Johnny! Quick!"

Seconds later, the footsteps pounded up the stairs. The commotion above increased in volume, shouts and bangs and crashes. *Was it a mutiny? Were they under attack?* Clara huddled by her crate, her knees protesting the prolonged stillness, every sense extended to try to determine the nature of the noises above, until her curiosity overwhelmed her and she finally rose to risk a peek toward the stairs.

A body lay awkwardly across the bottom steps. He was the loud man, she presumed. And by the amount of blood pooling beneath his chest, he was also very, very *dead*.

The noise above was becoming more frantic, and as time passed with no resolution to her present troubles, Clara was feeling quite anxious herself. Stuck in a cargo hold with grain that was gunpowder and a dead body to boot. She was at a complete loss. Nothing in her life had prepared her for an airship battle over the English countryside. A bubble of hysterical laughter escaped as she wondered what her etiquette instructor might say. Likely something about grace under pressure and that one's resolve could be seen in one's spine, but also that *ladies* would not find themselves in such a mess to begin with. She caught herself questioning her decision to leave the island for the first time since she had determined it to be the best course of action. She was completely out of her element. How could she ever have thought that her venture would be successful? She worried that she was a fool. Was this the end of her journey? Lost in an airship battle before she truly lived? Clara forced herself to take deep breaths to calm her racing heart. *No,* she thought. This was her choice and she would find a way through. She would do whatever necessary.

She unconsciously straightened her posture as she waited for some sign of the situation above. More information was needed before she could logically proceed. She would act when she had a better understanding of her circumstances. Until then, she would hide and wait.

The frenzy above gave way to a cacophony of whoops and hollers. Someone was cheering, but was the airship won or lost? The shouts were closer now but still too indistinct to interpret. A door banged open and someone crashed down the stairs, swearing an oath as he tripped over the dead man and scrambled further into the hold.

This is it, she thought.

Two more sets of footsteps came down, slow and

precise, but all the more intimidating for their measured pace.

"A captain in the cargo hold. You must be in a hurry to die. No true captain would abandon their pilots to carry on while hiding with the goods," a voice called. The voice was pleasant, aside from the underlying threat of imminent injury.

"You'll not be taking my ship today."

"You're sure about that?" called a woman's voice. "It looks as though I've got your sword right here. Pistols too. I'd say you're a little outmatched."

Clara peeked between the crates and caught a sliver of the standoff. White blouse, breeches, a tall boot, but she could not see the speaker.

"Shoot me then. I will not see my ship surrendered to pirates! The Tradists are closing in on your little operation, oh yes. Your misdeeds will catch up to you sooner than you think, be assured of that!"

"Well, Trick? Can I shoot him?"

"If you must. A coward's death for a coward captain."

Clara heard the pistol click into place, and realized the captain's plan. Throwing all caution to the winds, she scrambled to climb above the crates and yelled: "STOP!"

"By Victoria, there's a lady on board!" the woman swore, still aiming at the captain. The scene was frozen as each dealt with his or her respective shock. The man called Trick broke the silence.

"And what might your objection be? If you're feeling a bit delicate we can escort you above decks while we finish down here."

Clara found her voice, "No, not at all. Pardon me, but it's the gunpowder."

They stared.

"The crates behind him, they are filled with gunpowder, not grain. The hold is full of it. If you shoot him, you may blow the entire airship," she explained, as patiently as she could.

The woman narrowed her eyes while the man let out a deep belly laugh before whistling for others who quickly joined them in the hold.

"Well and you almost had us there, take him up and tie him well," he ordered, before turning back to her.

The captain was subdued, and escorted up the stairs, grumbling and spitting all the way. The man and woman stayed below, staring up at the girl in the stacks.

"Now my dear, what to do with you?"

Clara stared back at them, balancing on the crates. Their weapons were holstered now, but she did not hold illusions of her safety being secure under the current circumstances. The woman was tall, taller than the man beside her, though it was obvious that she deferred to his authority. Dark blonde hair was captured in a plait that hung past her waist. The man had a stocky build, with hair as dark as Clara's own. His open expression seemed capable of turning fierce or friendly, as he chose. She did her best to calm her breathing, calculating escape plans and dismissing them just as quickly. She was dependent on their good will. Clara figured that saving their lives was a good start. An act of trust would need to follow.

She carefully picked her way over the crates with as much dignity as she could muster in voluminous skirts and an over-sized jacket with a crowbar concealed in the sleeve. The man crossed the floor quickly to offer a hand to help her down. She elegantly dusted off her skirts, though the action made little difference to their sorry state, and waited for them to address her. As the silence dragged on her courage began to waver, and she decided the first introduction was to be hers.

"Good morning sir, madam. My name is Clara."

They stared.

They kept staring.

Would they ever stop staring?

The man cleared his throat. "Well then Miss… Clara, I'll be Patrick Kilarney, known to all as Trick. This here is Nessa."

"A pleasure to make your acquaintance, Mr. Kilarney, Mistress Nessa."

More silence. Nessa shifted her wide stance, a hand still resting on one of her holsters, "No offense, Miss, but I haven't seen many pilots in evening wear and most guests don't bunk in the cargo hold."

Clara could understand the confusion. She had not had time to change out of her ball gown, and the skirts were rather worse for wear. Her brother's coat was just a tad too large for her despite their similar, slender builds. She probably made quite a sight in the present moment.

"Well I can settle that for you, I'm a stowaway."

Both Trick and Nessa's eyebrows shot up. "A stowaway? Well," he scratched his head. "I suppose we are at your service Miss Clara, for saving the ship and all." His broad grin was at odds with the large sword at his side, but friendly all the same.

"Hold on, how do we know she's being truthful about the gunpowder? She seems clever enough to make a story of it," Nessa asked.

Clara raised a single brow at the challenge and allowed the crowbar to slide smoothly from her sleeve. Nessa took a quick step back and cocked a pistol at her. She gave the piratess her most gracious smile and went to the nearest crate, bracing herself to wedge it open. The front came off with a satisfying crack on her second attempt, revealing the barrels of gunpowder hidden within.

Trick grinned and pushed Nessa's pistol down, walking over to Clara and extending a hand.

"My thanks again, Miss."

"Yes, our thanks," said Nessa, with some reluctance before turning back to Trick, "But what are we going to do with her? Drop her off in the countryside?"

Clara considered her options. It was unlikely that the captured ship was bound for London.

"Might I ask where the ship is going? My plans are… adaptable, shall we say."

"Well we're not at liberty to share that information, but you can take it up with the Captain. Have no fear, he's an honourable man," Trick said. He offered her an arm and began to escort her towards the steps.

"Honourable, but a pirate, I presume?" she asked, finally giving voice to the word.

"I prefer the term 'liberator,'" a voice spoke from above.

Clara's gaze shot up. A tall man, lit from behind as his silhouette filled the doorway, his features obscured by shadow. One hand rested casually on the hilt of a slim sword. He walked down the steps into the hold, only pausing to allow Nessa time to drag the corpse aside. As the light of the portholes caught his face, Clara did her best to remain composed. His hair was a fiery red, spilling over his shoulders in a manner that was almost obscene. His sternness was almost overcome by the hint of dimples at his cheeks, but there was a dangerous amusement in his eyes and mouth.

"Trick, I see you have found a debutante."

"A stowaway, Captain."

"A stowaway debutante? How curious."

"She saved us all, sir, warned us about the gunpowder in the hold."

"I see. What a happy concurrence," he said, stepping closer to her. "We are in your debt Miss—"

"Clara. Just Clara," she spoke at last. He reached for her hand and bent in a sweeping bow to kiss it.

Trick grinned, "Miss Clara, may I present to you, the *Captain Duke.*"

Chapter 2: In which our heroine meets a legendary figure

The Captain Duke!

Clara had heard of this man. His name was whispered in all the major ports, with more rumours of his exploits and motivations than one man ought to inspire in a lifetime. However, in Clara's estimation, he couldn't be more than thirty years of age. As the three escorted her to the deck above, she adjusted her appraisal. In the clear light of day he looked even younger.

Her attention was distracted by the activity on the decks. Pilots were sorting and counting the goods while others watched over the imprisoned crew and captain. The ship's large oblong balloon towered over them, secured to the metal ship with heavy chain netting. A second airship was secured alongside the first, smaller and sleeker than the merchant vessel. This one had polished decks of light wood. Each tier of the deck was sculpted to break the high winds, rising as one moved astern with staircases curving up along each side. Large multi-paned windows lined the hull, and three smaller balloons held it aloft, tied together with rope and canvas. Propellers were spaced evenly along its sides, designed for swift navigation. Its delicate scrollwork made the utilitarian cargo ship seem ugly and corpulent by comparison.

The Captain Duke barked orders to his crew as they ran between the decks, transferring supplies with ingenious rope and pulley systems that Clara wished she had time to examine more closely. Instead, she hurried to keep up. He stopped in front of a bridge of knotted rope stretched between the two ships.

"Will you require assistance?"

Clara tore her eyes from the gap to meet the challenge in his eyes. She took a breath. If she was going to talk her way onto his ship she would need to prove she was capable. Steeling herself, she reached down to remove her boots. Passing them to the rather flustered Trick, she gathered her skirts and stepped out onto the bridge, steadying herself with the ropes stretched alongside. She was surprised to find it sturdier than many of the fence posts she had balanced on as a youth. The wind tore at the flaps of her jacket and the gauzy material of the dress, and the slightest glimpse from the edge of her sight of the land far below set her heart racing. Once again she cursed the circumstances that had prevented more suitable attire, but her feet were sure upon the ropes. She crossed the span between the ships with her head held high and jumped down to the other deck.

She braced herself against the wind as she waited for the Captain and Trick to finish crossing. The Captain acknowledged her with a nod and the barest tease of a grin, then immediately set about shouting orders to the crew. Trick clapped her on the back and handed her the boots.

"Thank you Mr. Kilarney, I wasn't sure I could spare a hand for them while I crossed."

"It was no problem at all. These are lovely boots for the land to be sure, but we'll fit you with some good deck slippers soon enough. You did well, Miss Clara."

"Just Clara, please."

"Very well, Clara, if you'll do me the honour of addressing me as Trick." He folded himself into an elaborate bow. She reciprocated with a formal curtsy, sweeping her skirts back and bending so gracefully that her etiquette instructor would certainly have cried with joy.

"The honour is mine, Trick."

He blushed. And blushed further still, upon discovering the Captain with arms crossed beside him.

"If the introductions are complete, Clara, Nessa, you will join me in my cabin. Trick, the ship is yours."

He turned and stalked toward a door at the rear of the ship. She received an unnerving smile from Nessa that did nothing to set her at ease, and the two of them followed behind.

The cabin held both work and living quarters. The half presently occupied by the trio was dominated by a table covered with maps. A correspondence desk took over the far corner. The morning light streamed into the room from a wall of large windows, slanting over the papers on the table. A number of shelves were lined with books and rolls of what Clara presumed to be more maps, all held secure by intricate wooden lattice. To her right was a wall dividing the cabin, with curtains pulled back from an arch leading into a bedroom. She could just catch a sliver of rumpled sheets through the opening, but quickly turned her attention back to the man clearing papers from the table. He pulled up a chair and gestured for her to do the same. Nessa leaned against the wall, observing them. Clara sat straight and met the Captain's gaze with what she hoped was a calm expression. Her composure was admittedly a bit rattled from the morning's events, and she had not had much opportunity for sleep. However, she was determined to find some logical solution to her troubles once she discovered the intentions of this Captain Duke. The standoff was finally broken by the Captain leaning forward and brushing his hair back from his eyes.

"Well, Clara, you have certainly made this venture more… surprising."

She was unsure how to respond so she waited in silence for him to continue.

"First, I must thank you. Your interference likely saved the lives of my crew, our cargo and myself as well."

"It was a happy accident, sir. Your good fortune coincided with my own."

"Your meaning?"

Clara decided honesty was her best advantage. She sensed no ill from this Captain… yet.

"Well, you see, the gunpowder was interfering with my plan of escape."

"Were you a captive then?"

"No, a stowaway, as Trick said. I boarded the airship with the assistance of my— a friend, and his glider. I thought I might hide in one of the crates, but the prohibited nature of the cargo was an unexpected obstacle."

"I see. And what circumstances brought about your fortuitous presence?"

Now she hesitated, unsure of how much to reveal.

"Reluctance is understandable," he continued. "Not many would turn stowaway without good reason. I only ask because your appearance would suggest a more unusual story than most."

Clara refused to blush, but smoothed her skirts self-consciously.

"I was hoping to find more reasonable attire in London," she offered.

"I have an extra pair of trousers that might fit her. They will do for now," Nessa spoke up, still leaning against the wall. Clara turned to her with gratitude, breaking her composure. It was the first sign of the possibility for a good rapport with the piratess.

"Oh would you? Excellent! I can pay of course, but really it would be such a favour…" she trailed off. "That is – thank you. It would be greatly appreciated."

Nessa smiled and with a nod from the Captain she went in search of the apparel. Clara's feelings were mixed between her relief at the prospect of changing out of her vexatious gown and her acute awareness of being left alone with the Captain Duke. A patch of sunlight illuminated his shoulder. His hair was bright against his shirt, and Clara cursed herself for noticing. She stilled herself into calm silence once more. The Captain continued to observe her.

"Correct me please, but I assume that to be a dress of some quality."

"Once, perhaps, but as you can see my adventures have spoiled it somewhat."

He raised an eyebrow, waiting.

"I had to leave in a bit of a hurry, you see…"

He waited still. Clara sighed.

"Fine, what is it you wish to know."

"Did you steal that jacket?"

"What? No, Archie gave it to me. I could hardly run away in naught but a ball gown."

"Archie?" he asked.

She went silent, cursing herself for the slip.

"I can assure you that anything you reveal will be kept in the strictest confidence. I am only trying to ensure the safety of my crew from reprisal over your presence on my ship. Do you fear imminent discovery of your escape?"

"I… I left with the consent of my family. My brother, Archie, had the idea for the airship. I did not have much time to prepare. There is a possibility that someone may be searching, but they will look to Europe first."

He considered this new information, leaning back in his chair.

"I realize my presence may be inconvenient, but my identity would perhaps be most secure aboard your vessel. I lack experience, but I could be of assistance to you and your crew."

The Captain Duke raised his brows, "You want to be a piratess?"

"A liberator, I believe you said."

He smiled then, showing a glimmer of white teeth.

"Yes, I did. What would compel a lady of your status to become a pilot?"

"What would compel a Duke to pilot a pirate ship?"

He laughed at that, and her stomach flipped at the boldness of her inquiry. This was a dangerous man, though it was difficult to remember that fact when he seemed so young and full of amusement. Her heart was pounding, but it was excitement, not fear, that drove her. This was an adventure she was compelled to chase. She was certain this airship was where she was meant to be. The moment was broken as Nessa returned with the promised clothing.

"Touché," he answered. "What are you prepared to offer in exchange to join my crew?"

Clara stood, taking courage from Nessa's renewed presence. She drew back her brother's coat and fiddled with the ties that bound the satchels beneath her skirts. The fullness of the gown concealed them well, and now it served to adequately preserve her modesty as she undid a second set of ties. She placed the satchels on the table with a heavy thud and removed the contents, relishing the open astonishment of Nessa and the Captain Duke. Two large coin purses, four slender books, and a matched set of dueling pistols were added to the table, along with the small packet of food. She added an extra apple from her pocket and a slim knife from her sleeve. She smiled sweetly at the Captain, his amusement quite apparent.

"Welcome aboard, Clara."

Chapter 3: In which our hero acquires a new pilot

The girl stood smiling over her stash of goods. The Captain Duke could not help but admire her, bold as brass, coming armed onto his ship. Nessa went pale as smoke at her failure to check the girl for weapons, and now her fingers twitched at the handle of her sword. He waved her off. The girl was no threat. Instead, he leaned forward and looked over the books on the table. One in particular caught his eye.

"*The Press and the Public Service*, by Grenville-Murray? That's an interesting text for a lady to be carrying on her... person."

"Really? I find questions on the modernization of diplomacy to be entirely relevant to one's education. This is most certainly a definitive work of Grenville-Murray's, I find it to be much more concise in outlining his politics than the assorted articles in *Household Words* or *The Morning Post*," Clara replied. He raised a brow.

"I was under the impression that *Embassies and Foreign Courts* was more relative to his career in diplomacy."

"Yes, but in this text, written later in his career, he expands upon his views of filling the diplomatic ranks by merit and skill rather than patronage. It is quite compelling," she added.

The Captain Duke did his best to maintain a neutral expression. Reaching over, he slid the small book and one of the coin purses towards his side of the table.

"This will be payment for your commission as a pilot on my ship. Are these terms acceptable to you?"

"Oh, yes!" she said. Nessa cleared her throat in disapproval. Clara corrected herself, "Yes, Captain."

"Nessa will show you to your new duties. You are dismissed."

He managed to keep a straight face while Clara attempted to replicate Nessa's smart salute. She quickly stuffed the remainder of her things into the satchels, including the shirt and breeches procured by Nessa. The two women left, with Clara following eagerly behind. Nessa glared at him, but spoke not a word as she shut the cabin door.

Alone now, he sighed deeply and reflected on the morning's strange turn of events. A new pilot. A rare text. A stowaway debutante. He hoped that he wouldn't regret his decision, but he trusted his gut and his instincts told him that Clara could be a valuable asset to his crew. She was a queerly clever girl, and dauntless despite her apparent inexperience in the world. If she was as she seemed, he was certain she would prove to be quite capable. If she was false, however… he refused to complete the thought. He picked up the book and perused the first few pages. This was certainly a day of surprises.

A knock at the door interrupted his study. Trick walked into the cabin.

"Captain? I have the inventory." He cleared the table,

pulling a ledger from the shelves above the desk.

"We can add a text, a purse and a pilot to that list of the goods cleared today."

"Which text, sir? I already have the pilot noted down," Trick smiled. The Captain gave him a hard look.

"Pardon me for being eager. Miss Clara did save our lives today. I saw her tailing Nessa and figured she'd found herself a commission."

"Well I had to find something for her and I doubt she would have taken to being left at the next port. Strange girl, that one."

"Indeed," Trick's eyes glittered for a moment before resuming their seriousness. "Now, if you'll observe here, their inventory lists don't match up at all. Only four crates of grain in total, with about 20 extra sacks scattered about to keep up the illusion. The other 56 are filled with barrels of smuggled gunpowder, as far as we were able to ascertain."

"Did the captain name his client? The reasons for the covert transportation?"

"No, sir, we checked the records and the names are a dead end. All are listed under a John Smith at a false address. He claimed a clerical error at first, and then admitted that he took the cargo for twice the normal rate for transportation with no questions asked."

"It's not one of ours, but what would the Tradists need with smuggled powder? They control the imports already."

"Not for me to say, Captain. I'd recommend sending out a few subtle inquiries, see if it was any other's business we weren't informed of. The Widow might know."

"The Black Widow? If you think it worthwhile then I'll write to her, but I trust that she would have sent word already if she'd heard anything. Meanwhile, what do you recommend for the Tradist ship? I don't enjoy the idea of traveling with explosives. We needed that grain. We'll be targeting another shipment before we dock."

"I've set Robbie to it; he can take the powder back to the Haven to be kept safe until we decide what to do with it."

"And the captain?"

"That coward? He knew what it was, sir, he led us straight down there. He would have blown the whole ship and us with it. A few surrendered, they ought to be spared, but in my opinion sir, he's unfit to call himself pilot."

"Tell Robbie to take them by way of the cliffs. The crew may take their gliders. The captain can swim for his."

"I'll pass the order along. Anything else, Captain?"

He considered the rest of the inventory list.

"The larder of the ship was especially well-stocked. It looks like our coward might have spent some of his ill-gotten profits a little early. Leave some of the goose for Robbie and his boys, bring the rest over. We'll have a feast tonight, officers and crew."

"Excellent idea, sir. A perfect way to welcome our new pilot."

"That is not— we already—" he sighed. "That is not my intention. We need to keep up morale for the next raid. None were lost today but that could change."

"Yes, Captain, of course. I'll spread the word. 'Morale' dinner tonight." He turned to leave.

"And Trick?"

"Captain?"

"Perhaps some entertainment might contribute to morale."

His smile grew even wider, "I'll warm up the squeezebox, sir!"

The Captain returned to updating the ledgers, noting down the name and year of the new book for his collection. After a moment, he added the source.

Clara — , Pilot, July 25th 1886.

Chapter 4: In which our heroine finally gets to wear trousers

Clara could hardly believe her good fortune as she followed Nessa from the cabin. She could not have foreseen such luck in her plans for escaping the island. A commissioned pilot on a renowned airship! Admittedly, the esteemed Captain Duke and his crew had a reputation as pirates, but she was certain there was more to that tale than was commonly known. He seemed to show more concern for the missing grain than the gunpowder gained in the raid. In any case, she already felt a rapport growing with Trick; a good sign of things to come. As for the Captain, it remained to be seen. He was a harder man to read. She was not yet sure whether he was humouring her for his own amusement, or if he was impressed by her capabilities. Nessa was another mystery. She could sense the other woman's unease. Clara was determined to prove herself. She had bought her way onto this airship, and now she would earn her place on it.

She followed Nessa across the decks and down a set of stairs into the crew's quarters below. The room they entered was a comfortable size, but nowhere near large enough to fit all of the pilots she had seen working above.

"These are the women's quarters," Nessa replied, seeing Clara's questioning look. "The Captain Duke was kind enough to let us have our own space. Easier to avoid problems among the crew."

"I see. Are there often... problems?"

"No, our crew knows its business. We're professionals. Colleagues. If any decide to take a lover they know it has to be done right by both parties."

Clara blushed, trying to control her reaction to Nessa's blunt speech.

"No, I didn't mean – ," she took a breath and caught the teasing glance Nessa cast her way as she struggled to compose her words. "I'm unfamiliar with airships. I was unsure whether it was standard for female pilots to have their own quarters."

"Some do. Our crew is pretty respectful. We're more like a family than most. The Captain Duke sets the tone and any who don't like it can leave. There's more lady pilots out there today than when I started, but there's still crews who hold to old seafaring superstitions about women on board."

Clara walked around the room. A small dresser and mirror were bolted securely in the corner. Of the twelve bunks, only four were bare. Nessa crossed to a closet and pulled out extra bedding.

"Well? Pick one and get dressed, we've got a lot to cover today if you're going to be one of my pilots."

Clara quickly stored her belongings in the cubby hole next to one of the few remaining top bunks and hurried to remove her dress. In her haste she knotted the laces and had to ask for Nessa's assistance. After a few moments of struggle, she happily agreed to Nessa's offer of a knife instead. It was rather satisfying to cut through the ribbons and lace. The pale blue fabric fell gracefully to the floor and she kicked it aside as she slipped into breeches and a loose tunic. She paused and took a deep breath. Her chest expanded fully and she breathed out a sigh of pleasure, sharing a small grin with the piratess. A loose leather girdle and supple boots completed her ensemble. She quickly rebraided her hair to keep it from her face. While looking around for a fastener, Nessa grinned and cut a swathe from the ruined gown. Clara appreciated the symbolism as she bound the end of her dark plait with the blue fabric. They hung her brother's coat in a second closet that was filled with various costumes and street clothes. Nessa explained that the dresses were for days when they docked in towns that were less receptive to women in breeches. Clara hardly recognized the woman she glimpsed in the mirror. It was odd to wear breeches, but she enjoyed the transformation they evoked.

"Alright, we'll take you on a tour now before you start your duties. I'm not entirely sure what the Captain wants you to be doing but I'm sure Trick will find something. What are you skilled at anyhow?"

"Well, I have been educated, if that's what you mean. I'm sure I can learn quickly."

Nessa pursed her lips.

"Do you know ropes? How to tie knots?"

"N-no, not really."

"Can you cook?"

"Well, I could certainly assist, I'm sure, but I don't have much practice."

"Can you climb?"

"Oh, yes. I think so. When I was little I used to climb the fences and trees around our property."

"Can you fight?"

"Fight?"

Nessa sighed. "Yes, fight. You're aboard an airship, not a leisure cruise. Can you fly at least?"

"Yes, I can fly. My brother took me on his glider any chance we had. I can definitely fly."

"Alone or just in pairs?"

"Well, as a pair, but I'm sure I can do it myself, really!"

Clara was becoming desperate as Nessa grew more and more cross. Perhaps this wasn't such a change in her fortunes after all. Clara took a deep breath. She could do this, she knew it, but how to prove herself when she had never had the opportunity to try? She squared her shoulders and looked Nessa in the eyes.

"I was tutored by the renowned Master Thompson alongside my brother. I learned every text on diplomacy and the British politic in my father's library by heart. I studied modern justice and the British common laws after Father found me cleaning out his dueling pistols at nine years of age because a boy stole a kiss and offended me. I speak English, German, French, and a little Flemish. I am schooled in both letters and numbers and I can recite passages from Machiavelli as easily as I can recount Spenser or Shakespeare. I climbed the tallest trees on the Island and taught myself to swim in a pond when I was six so that I could chase the ocean waves on our next trip to the seaside.

I have never truly fought an opponent, I prefer the use of my wits to violence, but I am practised in the defensive arts. My father did eventually permit me to train with firearms though I have never used them against another person."

She took another breath and would have continued, but she noticed that Nessa was barely concealing her mirth.

"It's certainly an impressive resume. Tell me though, what happened to the boy who stole the kiss?"

"Nothing," Clara grumbled. "They made me begin etiquette lessons with Miss Ellington instead."

The laughter came rolling from her now.

"I can – aha, I can just imagine a governess trying to manage a child like you. It explains a great deal though."

"Like what?"

"Well, you're such a lady when you're on the defensive. Cold, composed and the like. But there's some kind of hellcat ready to be unleashed under those braces. The hellcat I can work with. The lady may be of use as well someday. You'll do fine."

Clara blushed at the other woman's praise. They shook hands. Then Nessa clapped an arm around her shoulders and steered her out of the room. They almost ran right over Trick who had just come around the corner.

"I see you two are thick as thieves already."

"Liberators, dear Trick. The Captain says no thieving aboard his ship."

"Yes, yes, well he's instructed me to inform the crew

that the most recently liberated bounty is enough to warrant a feast tonight."

Nessa raised an eyebrow, but Trick only winked in return.

"Well," said Nessa after a moment. "We had better get you up to speed Clara. Tonight you'll get a true taste of what it means to be one of our pilots. You've got to work for your supper on this airship. I hope you can dance or sing."

"Oh yes, Miss Ellington insisted." They shared a grin at Trick's look of confusion.

Nessa linked her other arm into Trick's and the three of them set off to the main deck. Clara could feel a sense of elation spreading throughout her. She was ready to begin her adventure.

Hours later, Clara was positive that she had never been so tired or pleased in her life. Her body was unused to the vigour required for life in the air, but the cool winds whipping her face and the sight of the whitest of clouds stretching out over the land to kiss the sea thrilled her to no end. She paused to sweep some loosened strands of hair from her eyes. She would have to learn to braid her hair like Nessa next time. The expert pilot's long, blonde hair never escaped its fastening.

"How are ye there?" shouted Cat, another of the pilots. She and her brother, Mouse, had joined the crew as practically babes. Their father had been a captain and raised them on his airship after their mother's passing. When he died, the two of them had sought out the Captain on their own. The bold little Catherine and her timid younger brother, Morris, were two of the best climbers and gliders she had ever met. Not that she had met many, but at 14 and eight years of age their reputations were assured.

"Quite fine, thank you," Clara called back over the wind. Still, she felt a stab of anxiety as Cat ran nimbly across the rope bridge beneath the balloons.

"We'll teach you to glide tomorrow when we're over water. You seem to take to the heights well."

They were standing on a small platform suspended from the ropes above and connected to the deck by a tightly woven ladder.

"Would it concern you if I was actually quite terrified by the prospect of falling?"

Cat answered with a grin.

"You'd be a fool if you weren't, and we can't have fools up here. Right, Mouse?"

Her brother swung down from his post checking the ropes that secured the balloon. He landed perfectly with a wide grin, and Clara laughed at their antics.

"You'll feel better once you know how to fly. You'll never take to solid ground again," he answered. "The weather looks good for tomorrow. We'll teach you."

"Well with such expert instructors I can hardly refuse the opportunity."

Mouse blushed, as only a young boy can, and puffed out his chest with pride. Cat punched his arm.

"Aw, you're blushing at the lady now!"

"Am not! She just said we're expert!"

"Are too!"

"Am not!"

Clara recalled the secondary explanation for the siblings' nicknames. Just as quickly as their squabble had started, it switched to a challenge to see who could reach the main deck first. Clara carefully made her way down as she watched the two of them race to another ladder, each scrambling down a side of it like a rope. By the time she reached the bottom, they were squabbling again over who had won and who had cheated. She was breathless with laughter, but quickly composed herself when the Captain Duke brushed past her to separate the two of them.

"She cheated, she jumped at the end!"

"He could have too! He was only ahead by a smidge 'cause he got to the ladder first, that's all."

"I was watching and I declare it a tie. Any questions?" he asked, crossing his arms.

"No sir," they replied together.

"Wash up without fighting and there's an extra serving of duck for each of you."

They scrambled off below deck, shouting their thanks behind them.

"Quite the pair, aren't they?" Clara spoke aloud, addressing the Captain. She had hardly seen him since receiving her commission that morning. He chuckled in reply,

"They've each grown a foot this week, I'd swear on it. And you've never seen anyone tuck away food the way they do. They've got hollow bones like the gulls."

He laughed, then checked his composure, smoothing out his long blue coat.

"How are you taking to the pilot's life?"

"Quite well. Nessa taught me the knots today, Trick said I may assist him with the ledgers, and those two have just shown me how to climb. I'm to fly soon as well."

"Good. Please excuse me, I need to speak with Trick."

He left, and Clara stood there, bemused by the sudden change in his attitude and his hasty exit. Nessa called her over to the foredeck and she hurried to meet her.

"What did you say to the Captain?"

"Just what I learned today."

Nessa's frown turned into a sly grin and a look of mischief crossed her face.

"Hmm, perhaps we'll find out more at dinner. You did well today, Clara. Our crew works hard for their ship and for each other. We're a family. You'll have to decide whether you're one of us soon." She stopped Clara's protest, "Not now. Right now you love the adventure, and I know it. The skies are freedom to you and I, and there's a world of possibility up here. But, I need to know that you'll still be with us in the hard times as well. I won't ask what you're running from. Just prove to us that you're not still running."

Nessa steered her down to the cabin to wash, silencing all of Clara's questions with another rambling stream of stories and instructions about life aboard the airship.

Chapter 5: In which our heroine sups aboard an airship

Below deck, Cat was already in the room along with some of the other female crew. Clara was suddenly shy at the prospect of meeting all of her new roommates. Never before had she lived with so many women of such varied occupations. Three were regular pilots, one worked in the kitchens, and the final two were nurses. They all welcomed her warmly, passing her a bottle of rum and laughing at her expression as she tasted it. Cat took the bottle next, to Clara's shock. She moved to take a swig but was stopped by a stern look from Nessa.

"Oh come now. I'm nearly 15, practically an old maid!"

"Your birthday was only in June, child, and the summer is not yet over. Besides, moderation is a virtue. Captain's rules. You get a pint at dinner and not a sip more until you're older."

Cat drew herself to her full height but the older woman towered over her. Nessa was almost the height of the Captain, and taller than many of the male pilots as well. The young girl rolled her eyes before returning the bottle with a flourish. Nessa grabbed her up in a hug that left her feet dangling a foot off the floor.

"Where did my little Cat get to?"

Clara basked in the warm glow of such informal female companionship. She had a similar sort of familiarity with her own brother, but had little experience with other women. At home, gentler activities and distractions had ruled their social calendar. She quickly chased away her ruminations with a second drink, not better than the first but she was prepared for the burning taste this time.

"You'll be a true pilot after tonight, Clara!" one of the cooks shouted. Maggie, perhaps? Or was that one Peg and the nurse Maggie? No, that one was definitely Charlotte, she thought, trying to keep the introductions straight as the warmth spread through her. The women shared their stories and advice and boasted of their feats on board the airship. All seemed to agree that the Captain flew the best ship and Clara was fortunate to have fallen in with them. None appeared to have any reservations about living their lives as pirates. One, a nurse named Susan, began a tale of medicines delivered to an Irish village but the others stopped her at the graphic description of the disease. Finally, a bell rang from above and the women made their way to the mess hall, Cat running full-tilt ahead of them.

They entered the warm, brightly-lit room to the smell of roasted duck, fresh bread, and a steamy summer vegetable stew. Clara's stomach growled audibly. She had only had a light lunch before setting about her lessons that day, and between the demanding labour and the intoxicants she was more than ready for a warm meal. The men of the crew shouted greetings across the room and the pilots quickly mingled. Everyone came over to welcome Clara, and Cat was beaming with excitement as she took charge of the introductions.

"This is Sully, Mouse says he snores but he's the best at navigatin' over the water 'cause he was a sailor before he came up as a pilot. This is Darion, he's a fighter, but he's ticklish too so don't let him bother ye. This is Cook. His name is something else but we call him Cook. Peg helps him in the galley."

Clara stifled her laughter at the colourful introductions, and greeted each of them in turn. It soon became apparent that Nessa spoke true: They were a family, teasing and joking and sharing stories of each other's feats and foibles. They were a happy, boisterous group.

A few thumps on the table silenced the crowded room as they turned their attention to the front of the room. The Captain Duke stood tall in a long blue dress coat, with an empty mug turned gavel in one fist. Mouse ran over with a jug of foamy beer to fill it. His serious expression curled into a brief smile of thanks.

"Tonight we celebrate another successful raid on the Tradists. None were lost and much was gained." The Captain gestured towards the galley door, where Beatrice and the other kitchen staff entered bearing platters and dishes piled high with food. He paused for the cheers, and then raised a hand for silence as he continued,

"We have more work to do before joining Robbie and the others, but tonight we celebrate a job well done."

He raised his glass and all joined in the toast that followed:

To the winds, to the clouds, to a life lived well,
Take me up to the sky!
To the heavens above and the land far below,
Pilot, keep to the sky!
To the sun on your face and the stars in your eyes,
Captain! Give me the sky!

They drank deeply to the toast, then chaos resumed as the meal began in earnest. The food was heavenly. Clara was surprised to learn of the facilities on board. It was a first-class airship. They were able to restock their larder more frequently than boats, and so fresh food was readily available. The bread was even made on board, thanks to the expert labours of Cook and his staff. Nessa explained that the Captain didn't believe in keeping his pilots half-starved while he and the officers ate their fill. They regularly ate with the crew themselves. Nessa took a seat on the bench beside Clara, with Cat supplanting a heavily mustachioed pilot to claim her other side. She was enjoying her meal and the conversations around her, but her eyes strayed to observe the Captain as he strolled about the room. Nessa noticed her inattention, and leaned over to whisper,

"He'll get his plate last, there's more than enough."

"Oh, I wasn't–," Clara blushed. "It's a lovely coat," she finished, picking at her food. Nessa was blessedly merciful, pretending it was a perfectly legitimate excuse for her fixation. In truth, it was a fine blue coat that perfectly set off his hair, now tied back with a dark ribbon. The candlelight made it look like a seam of fire down his back.

"He stole it off of one of the first Tradist ships he raided, you know? It was a gnarly old captain in charge, one of those used to the days of the East India Company. He kept Orientals as indentured servants and charged double to the Irish towns. A meaner soul you never saw. So, the Captain Duke, he takes his share of the cargo and leaves the airship to the Orient pilots, right? And before he flies off, the other captain – tied up on his own ship, you see, and expecting to be taken for ransom – he calls out, 'Aren't you forgetting something?' The Captain Duke turns about and tells him he's right. And he calls for the pilots to toss over that fine blue jacket that he's wearing now. It was far too big for him back then, but he's grown into it well don't you think?"

"How long has he been a... a liberator then?" Clara asked.

"Since he was about Cat's age I think. Maybe younger. Don't let his age fool you though; he's one of the cleverest Captains I ever served. I have nothing but respect for the man."

"Have you known him long?"

"I've been here seven years, just a touch longer than Cat and Mouse. Trick's known him the longest, been his first mate from the start. He says he took one look and knew he was a 'lad to be followed,' even though he has more than a few years on the Captain. They named me their bosun within my first year."

"Were you always a pilot?"

"No, I was apprenticed to a dressmaker once. I ran off with a pilot who caught my eye, and decided I liked his stories of life in the clouds better than I liked the man who told them. So I joined up. Or I tried to. It took a while to find a ship with the right fit," she said with a wink.

"And a pirate ship was your choice?" Clara asked, laughing.

"Hey, you're a piratess yourself now. Or you will be as of the next raid. But yes, I find that the Tradists are rather old-fashioned when it comes to respecting a woman's abilities. You should ask the Captain about his philosophy of liberation sometime. Or you'll figure it out soon enough. 'Pirate' is in the eye of the beholder."

"I suspected as much."

"We know. It's probably why he allowed you to join our crew. We're not the most exemplar of her Majesty's subjects, but we have our own code and we stick to it."

Clara chewed as she considered Nessa's words. She was right, she wouldn't have joined them, gunpowder or not, if she hadn't sensed the friendship here. Pirates or liberators, or whatever they called themselves, these were good people, even if they had a rather liberal attitude toward the necessity of violence.

Her reverie was interrupted by a loud squawk of an accordion being warmed up. Trick was perched on a tall stool at the front of the room.

"Oh good! You're in for a treat tonight," Nessa said, as she quickly mopped up the rest of her stew with a slice of bread. Cat was already out of her seat and racing to the front to sit with her brother at the first mate's feet. Clara hurried to finish her own supper as the entertainment began.

"Well what shall we have tonight?" Trick called. "A waltz? A libretto?"

"Tammany's jig!" shouted Cat and Mouse together.

"Tammany's jig? Are you sure?"

"Yes, sir!" replied Mouse. The boy was leaning forward, enraptured by the instrument.

"And what will you give for it?"

"A brass ring!" yelled Cat, as she fished it from her pocket and presented it to the first mate with a curtsy.

Trick put on the ring with a flourish, pausing to stroke the dark stubble on his face before assuming a gallant pose with one knee cocked. He launched into a rollicking tune, singing loudly in a beautiful tenor about a man named Tammany who danced for the Faerie Queen.

Tables and benches were soon cleared to make room for dancing. Trick managed to both play and dance, while others helped to carry the tune. It seemed many of the pilots had favourites they were more than eager to share. Clara held back at first, unused to the wildness of the dancing, but she was soon pulled in by Cat and the steps were not too difficult to learn. It became apparent to her that any skill at courtly dancing paled in comparison to the talents of the crew. Trick and Nessa danced a jig together in the Irish style, leaping and spinning about the room. One of the dark-skinned pilots jumped upon a table for a dance of his own people. Clara was fascinated, and wished she could be as bold one day. She was out of breath and glowing from the dancing when Trick called out to her.

"Alright, alright. Miss Clara, it's your turn now!"

Her refusal was already upon her lips when she caught the Captain watching her from across the room.

"Well? What will it be?" Trick pressed.

With the entire room's attention on her, Clara lifted her chin and answered, "I don't know many of these tunes. I can sing 'In the Gloaming' if it pleases you."

Trick raised an eyebrow, and smiled widely as he agreed. They cleared space for her in the centre of the room. Trick took the opportunity to rest on the stool as he played. The crew settled down and with the lanterns casting a soft light about the hall, Clara began to sing the familiar tune.

In the gloaming, oh, my darling!
When the lights are dim and low,
And the quiet shadows falling
Softly come and softly go.

She walked slowly as she sang, circling Trick with his accordion, addressing the entire room. Her singing had been her saving grace for Miss Ellington to continue with her etiquette training. Despite all her faults she did have a lovely voice.

In the gloaming, oh, my darling!
Think not bitterly of me!
Tho' I pass'd away in silence,
Left you lonely, set you free.
For my heart was crush'd with longing,
What had been could never be;
It was best to leave you thus, dear,
Best for you and best for me.

Clara almost faltered as she finished the song. She made the mistake of looking to the Captain, and the intensity of his gaze had her feeling suddenly quite self-conscious for singing a tale of love. She was determined not to show the effect he had, and sang the final lines to her accompaniment.

Will you think of me, and love me?
As you did once long ago.

A pause of silence followed the final note of the instrument, followed by a rousing bout of applause. Trick swept her up in an embrace, before handing her a mug procured by Nessa. He shouted above the crowd,

"To Clara!"

"To Clara!" they answered, and the celebration resumed.

Clara was surrounded by well-wishers and her mug was soon empty from all the toasts and cheers. She murmured her thanks as she crossed the room to refill her cup. She had just extricated herself from Peg, Beatrice and another of the kitchen staff when she turned and almost knocked the Captain over. He steadied her with a smile and collected her mug to fill it himself. Clara accepted the drink with thanks.

"You sang well," he said.

Clara dabbed the extra foam from her mouth with the edge of her sleeve, feeling the blush growing on her cheeks.

They stood there a few moments longer, in silence. Clara sipped at her beer, and tried to think of something to say. The Captain took in the rest of the room, not meeting her eyes. She took the opportunity to observe him, his pale eyes reflecting the light from the lanterns as it played across his high cheekbones. She had heard tales of his exploits and rumours of dalliances with highborn ladies. She could see how his air of mirth and danger would fuel many ladies' fantasies. She was caught off guard when he turned to her.

"Why are you here?" he asked.

"I... well, you found me, and-"

"It seems almost too great of a coincidence."

Clara's mood darkened, "And what, exactly, is your meaning?"

The Captain was unmoved by her glare.

"Answer this riddle for me. A young woman of obvious high birth shows up in a cargo hold riddled with illegal ammunitions, in a tattered ball gown and a gentleman's coat. A woman who saves my crew but smuggles dueling pistols aboard my ship. Then, despite her absolute lack of qualification or experience, she purchases a pilot's commission rather than booking passage, and takes strikingly well to every task she is assigned." He set his beer down on a nearby table and crossed his arms. "You have befriended the crew, handle the ropes like a born pilot, and yet sing like an accomplished lady of the upper realms. Among your many assets, I hardly see the need to add a pirate's employment to your resume. You might be a Tradist spy, but if so, you make a rather poor one. I believe myself to be a good judge of character and while our encounter was, in all likelihood, a fortunate accident, I am still left with the mystery of why you have chosen the life of a pilot over that to which you were obviously born."

Clara's face burned.

"And what of yourself, sir?" she shot back.

"Myself?"

"Your reputation precedes you. The 'Captain Duke' who flies through the clouds, stealing ladies' hearts and Tradist cargo. A pirate, a liberator, whatever you call yourself, playing at Robin Hood with your band of Merry Men. And yet, also a titled Lord if rumours are to be believed. You are as much an enigma as I. Might I not keep a few secrets as well?"

He shifted his stance, crossing his arms with his hip cocked to the right, "As Captain, I take it as my duty to know whether you may endanger my crew."

"Then I will confirm what you suspect. I am no spy. I have left my birthright behind. I have a genuine desire to be part of your crew and I will work hard for my place in it."

"This is not some grand adventure to take back to your sitting room once you've had enough."

Clara glared at him. She was tired of his mercurial dealings. She drank deeply, finishing the mug of beer before passing it back to him.

"This is my choice. I no longer recognize that life. I have seen what becomes of those who force themselves to adhere to that path. Please respect my wish to determine the course my own shall take." She strode across the room as steadily as she was able and left for the upper deck.

Clara needed to feel the air upon her face. She had tasted the freedom of the skies, and no one – Captain or not – would take it from her again.

Chapter 6: In which our heroine finds a friend

The land below was cast in the deep shades of the night. A river gleamed with moonlight where its currents met. Clara could just make out the barest features of small houses far below as the ship followed its course through the stars. The air soothed her, brushing cool fingers across her face and neck as she stood at the railing. She let it blow her coat behind her, knowing she ought to keep warm, but enjoying the new sensations far too much to be sensible quite yet. The alcohol had gone to her head, she reasoned, trying to rationalize her reaction to the Captain. How had such a nice evening turned into a battle? She belonged here. She felt it in her soul. In less than a day she felt more at home on these decks than in any parlour. She would fight for her place, and the Captain would have to accept that. Clara puffed out a breath of exasperation. She should have handled the exchange better. He hadn't *really* accused her of anything, just pried into areas she'd rather left alone. She likely owed him an apology, and it made her pride sore to think of it. At a small noise behind her, she turned to find Nessa had joined her on the decks.

"Well hello, Miss Clara, I hope the fine evening air is treating you well," she teased, joining her at the rail and passing another bottle of the seemingly endless supply of intoxicants aboard the ship.

"Where on earth does it all come from?"

"Oh we don't always imbibe this much, but that last raid had a rather plentiful supply. That sneaky lout had definite plans for his ill-gotten gains."

They laughed and toasted each other, then sat with their backs to the rail and their legs stretched out in front of them.

"Tell me what's troubling you."

"I may have been a bit cross with the Captain. He has no trust in me."

"He only has the safety of his crew in mind. You're a new pilot. Untrained, unproven. I hardly trust you myself," she joked. Clara shot her a dark look.

"I told him he was playing at Robin Hood."

Nessa roared at that one. "Truth be told, I'm not sure it's the first he's been told that and I'm certain it won't be the last. It's good to see some of that hellcat coming out. Give it time. I still don't know how well you'll do in a raid, but I do trust that you'll work hard for your place here. The Captain will sort himself out."

"If he decides to let me stay."

"He'll come around. And he'll answer to me if he wants you gone. Our crew is short without Robbie and the others. I need hard workers," Nessa said, putting an arm around her shoulders. "Besides, I like your spirit."

"You are like the sister I never had. At least, if I had one, I'd want her to be like you," Clara said, returning the hug.

"That's sweet of you to say. I wonder what my own

sister might think sometimes."

"You have a sister?"

"And six brothers. I come from a good family but it was hard to find steady work for them all. I was born in the middle but took the lion's share of the work after our mother died. I worked at the clothier's until my sister was married off to a kind clergyman, then left her a note to say I was going to the Dominion of Canada and ran away with my fellow. I peeked in one day, years later. She had a baby in her lap and two young ones running around. She looked happy."

"You should write to her."

"And say what? I'd rather not pile more lies on the lies I have already told her. Perhaps she will forgive me for the first one someday."

"I think she would. My brother would never let a thing come between us."

"So your family will be missing you then?"

"No. Well, yes. It's complicated, but they know it was the right thing to do."

"They know where you've gone?"

"Not precisely. My brother helped me when I learned I would need to leave sooner than expected, but they knew it was always my intention to live my own life."

"Not a runaway then? What of your parents?"

"My father passed. Last spring. I'd rather not talk of my family, if you please."

Clara felt the unfamiliar stirrings of homesickness. She had left with her mother's reluctant blessing, but the sudden parting was none the easier for it.

"Did you dream of being a pilot?"

Nessa kindly changed the subject as they shared the bottle between them.

"I had every intention of finding some sort of engagement, likely as a governess of some sort, but to be perfectly honest, I was at a loss. My plan extended as far as getting off the island. I had no time for further considerations. I was quite glad when this opportunity presented itself."

"Well you're lucky we did present ourselves. London would have ate up a pretty girl like you without a second thought."

"I heard that London was a bastion of progress since the reforms."

"In some circles, to be sure. Not for those who are running away from the privileges they were born to. Queen Victoria has made remarkable progress in her campaign, but the elements that challenge her are ever present."

"What do you mean? I read that her reforms have had a positive reception throughout."

"That's the problem with learning only from books and reports. Words can reveal both truth and lies. You need to experience something to truly know it. When the ministers challenged her rule, she had to act to maintain her throne. Prince Albert's passing affected her greatly. The impact of her reforms was not understood at the time, and the rights they permitted may well be taken away again by the lawmakers. Her Majesty has even refused to endorse the enfranchisement of her sex. The fight for equalization and our right to vote continues, but the real work being done is by the women taking advantage to open their own laboratories, their shops and their schools. It cannot be done all at once, but little gains here and there go a long way. Down there we still need skirts to appear respectable. In the skies, thanks to men like the Captain, we are respected for our own merit."

"Yes, the great Captain Duke. Lord of the Skies," she grumbled.

"Perhaps it is time we give this bottle a rest for a while," Nessa said, laughing as she set it aside.

"What is his story anyway? Is he truly a Duke? What is he the Duke of?"

"That's his tale to tell. He is rather private about his own history." Nessa paused, leaning back against the rail before continuing, "There's some kind of a connection, Clara, between the two of you. Be mindful of it. He's not a man to be trifled with, but once you are in his confidence he will fight at your side through thick and thin."

Clara sighed and tilted her head back against the rail to stare at the stars. They seemed to circle against the black. She spoke of their dancing and Nessa laughed and helped her back to the cabin, forcing a few deep drinks of water along the way. Clara slept soundly in her bunk that night, and dreamt of flying.

Chapter 7: In which our hero regrets his egregious assumptions

He woke feeling like the greatest fool alive. The Captain Duke groaned as he rolled out of bed to retrieve the tincture of willow bark from the cabinet. He sat at his desk, rubbing the sleep from his eyes as he waited for it to take effect. He expected his crew to bear their responsibilities and so would he, headache or no. He was in a foul mood, and the lingering effects of last night's festivities were only partly to blame. He was certain that he had ruined the evening; an apology was definitely in order. He had lashed out at Clara with his accusations when there was little, if any, merit to them. He wished he could take back his words. She had an inconvenient effect on him. It wasn't entirely unwelcome, but he could not afford to let his interest complicate their collegial relationship. He tried to convince himself that she was just another pilot, but he was all too aware that the facts were otherwise. He pushed the mystery to the back of his mind. Even if Clara was out for her own tale of the Captain Duke, the reality of the difference in their stations could not be denied for long. He wondered if his own mythology was coming now to haunt him.

A knock on the door preceded the entrance of Trick, bearing a much-welcome plate of breakfast and strong coffee to wash it down. The Captain waved him over and started on the meal as Trick gave his report.

"The crew are feeling the effects, sir, but most are bearing it happily. It was good to give them reason to celebrate."

"Good to see it wasn't wasted on all," he grumbled as he drank deeply.

"Wasted? Not at all, everyone had a pleasant time," Trick responded cheerfully. Too cheerfully.

"And what is the reason for your good mood?"

"What is behind your unpleasant one?"

"It's none of your business."

"It is if you think I'm about to let you spoil all your good favour with the crew by storming around with a cloud over your head. Out with it."

The Captain glared, but he could not deny Trick's counsel.

"It's the girl."

"Clara?"

"Yes, what other girl? Of course I mean Clara."

His voice caught on her name and he scowled at his meal.

"She is quite an exceptional young lady. I see why she might have an effect on you but I cannot fathom why it would be a poor one."

"I... might have been rude last night."

Trick looked at him with shock and spoke in a rare fit of

anger, "Captain, I have never known you to make inappropriate advances, and you'd better not have started now. Clara is a proper young lady, and you will make any reparations necessary to keep her on this ship if she so chooses."

"Calm yourself, I did no such thing."

"Well then? What happened?"

"I might have inferred that she could be a spy."

"Inferred?"

"Accused, more like."

Trick sighed and rubbed his forehead.

"Ah, Captain. What am I to do with you?"

He chose not to answer, taking a large bite of breakfast instead.

"Well, what are you planning to do about it?"

The Captain swallowed and took a dainty sip of the coffee, "I plan to run my ship as I always do."

"And Clara…?"

"Is a pilot. An employee. I see no reason to press the matter further."

Trick sighed and paced the room. The Captain ignored him, studiously examining the cooling food as he ate. Trick gave another loud sigh and walked to the door. The Captain shoveled another bite into his mouth.

"Fine. Be stubborn. But she's a special one. You know

it, I know it. She's got some touch of destiny about her. You can't ignore it forever." Trick exited the cabin in a huff.

The Captain sat back and pushed the plate away. He was no longer hungry. Instead, he stared through the windows and thought over his options. It was dangerous to get close to the girl, but that did not prevent him from wanting to help her on her journey. The ship was big enough to avoid her; he could pass on requests through Trick and Nessa easily enough. Besides, after a few days of work on the ship she might decide to leave after all. A pilot's life was nothing like the grand tales told in parlour rooms. He figured she might make it through a single raid before quitting. Yes, that was it, one taste of their real work and Clara would be off at the nearest port. No good could come of a closer association, and a debutante was not cut out for the pilot's life. He washed himself and finished dressing. By the time he was ready to join his crew, the Captain Duke had convinced himself that she would likely be ready to leave that very day. Instead, he was greeted by shouts and hollers from the men and women gathered on the deck, all staring upwards. Craning his neck to see what they were looking at, he saw Clara high above, balanced on the glider deck.

She was strapped alongside little Cat, who appeared to be giving her some final instructions. Mouse was perched above them, monitoring the wind speed. A signal from him was all they needed to make the leap, plunging down along with his heart. He took a few panicked steps forward before catching his composure, and waited, breathless, as they curved out over the water and did a few laps around the ship. His stomach rolled into knots and he found he was glad he hadn't finished his breakfast after all. Still, as they soared by, his anxiety was overcome by the gliders' obvious joy. They were harnessed together, moving in tandem as they manoeuvered the wings, legs stretched out and hooked

53

into leather loops that controlled the tail wing. It was an older model that they used for training: more cumbersome, but sturdy. The lighter models used by his pilots required one's absolute concentration and complete control. The Captain watched as they circled. The delighted shouts of the two young women could be heard even over the loud encouragement from the crew. Finally, they turned in to land on the deck, releasing their legs and banking the wings to slow their descent. They found their feet with ease, unstrapping themselves and collapsing the wings of the glider before clasping each other in a great hug, Clara practically picking Cat off of the deck. Grinning ear to ear, they turned to give deep curtsies to the cheering pilots.

Nessa walked over to stand by the Captain, calling out, "Oh you're looking a little pale there, Captain. How did you like our morning lessons?"

"I had not realized it would be so soon."

"Oh, she insisted and Cat was all for it. She seems to have woken none the worse for the festivities last night. They came this morning as soon as we were over the water. This is their fourth run so far. Mouse claims she's a natural, but they want her to have more tandem practice before they'll let her take one out on her own."

"They've taken over her training, I see."

Nessa laughed, "Can you blame them? They're eager to have such a willing student. And she's been very respectful of their teachings, even despite their ages. She treats them like the experts they are."

A small smile crossed his lips before he caught it.

"Very well. As long as it doesn't interfere with their

work. Or the work of the crew."

"Yes sir, Captain. I'll get them back on task."

"And Nessa, we'll need to meet about the plans for the next raid. Have you had news from Robbie?"

"Safely at the Haven, his transmission came this morning. He made contact with a few sources that might have interesting leads for us."

"Excellent. We'll have an officers' meeting before dinner."

She gave him a salute before leaving to assign the crew their duties for the day. He saw Clara standing with Cat and Mouse, still glowing from the flight but listening with rapt attention as the young boy gave her instructions for her next attempt, gesturing wildly with his arms to mimic their flight. She nodded in understanding, and shook their hands, saying something that made the two young pilots glow with happiness. They ran off after Nessa pointed them to their tasks. He saw Clara smile after them. Then her eyes turned and caught his gaze. He tried to give a curt, friendly nod, but she held his gaze until Nessa caught her attention. She followed Nessa to the ropes without a second glance. The Captain sighed. This was going to be more difficult than he thought. He wanted her to succeed. He wanted her to stay. He wanted to teach her everything about his ship and watch as her face lit with that glow that came with mastering each new task.

He banished the thought before it could form completely, and went about his day. A captain could be very busy if he chose to be, and he decided the best course of action was to devote himself to the work at hand.

The next week proceeded without incident. When Clara was working on deck, he busied himself in his office. When she was assisting Trick with the bookkeeping, he found himself navigating or overseeing the work of the crew. When she had her gliding lessons, high above the decks, only then did he find reason to be somewhere he could watch her fly. He noticed that Clara's hands were raw from the ropes one night at the evening meal, and discreetly had Nessa place some extra lanolin oil in the women's cabin. He noticed that she struggled to reach some of the higher shelves and had the ledgers moved down. When they ran into each other at supper, the two exchanged nothing more than a comment on the fine weather before he hurried off with some excuse.

The time was approaching for their next raid and he was determined to keep her safely out of the way with Cat and Mouse. The two children complained every time, but accepted his verdict that they were not allowed on active raids until they were 16 and could best Nessa in training. He watched the clouds pass by the windows in his office until he heard Trick enter behind him, shutting the door quietly.

"Do you have the plans readied? Nessa will be joining us shortly," the Captain called without turning. Silence greeted him.

"Do you have them or no—" he cut off as he turned to discover Clara standing in his quarters.

"I'm sorry to bother you, Trick asked me to work on the ledgers."

"Oh. Of course," he stood straight, and inwardly swore at himself as he saw her eyes narrow.

"I can work on them another time if my presence

disturbs you," she said, with a dangerous lilt to her voice. The Captain saw the challenge too late and knew he was trapped.

"Not at all. Please, make yourself comfortable."

Clara walked by him with her chin in the air to pull one of the large, leather bound registers from the middle shelves. She sat at the desk in the corner and opened it to the page she had worked on last. Her neat handwriting was a great improvement over his first mate's crooked calligraphy. She knew a better form of double-entry accountancy and Trick had entrusted her with the task of transferring the inventory numbers. He went to busy himself with the maps and reading the latest missive from Robbie.

"I noticed you moved the books around. Thank you," she said.

He tried to think of a suitable reply, but a heavy silence dragged on until she interrupted his attempt.

"Nothing? Very well then."

"I beg your pardon?" he said with as much detachment as he could muster. He chanced a glance in her direction and found her half-turned in her chair, glaring at him. He felt his chest constrict. Gods, but she was a sight. Green eyes flashing, dark hair escaping its braid as always, long legs clad in breeches and tall boots. Her long coat she abandoned in the summer heat. She was absolutely captivating.

"You have hardly spoken to me this week."

"I have been occupied. A Captain has many duties."

She flushed at that. He was sorry for his sternness immediately after speaking.

"Forgive me. I was only wondering if you regret your decision," she said.

"Regret... which decision exactly?"

"To allow me on your ship. My pilot's commission. You are friendly to all and yet you make a point of ignoring me."

"I have done no such thing."

"You have so."

"Have I been impolite?"

"Not at all, your politeness is astounding."

"Then what is your concern?"

"It— You— I want to know why."

"Why? I am your Captain. I do not have the time to attend to every individual on my ship," he said carefully. He deliberately relaxed his posture, stretching his legs under the table as he turned back to his maps.

"And yet the ledgers appear to be rearranged."

"I meant to organize them long ago."

"So it was not because they were out of reach for your new bookkeeper?"

"It made more sense to place them on a lower shelf."

"And the lanolin oil?"

They glared at each other from their seats across the room. Why couldn't she let things be. Why must they discuss this all now, when he was so unsettled by her proximity. He was not a young lad anymore, and was no longer used to feeling quite so shaken around a woman.

"What of it?" he asked. She gave him a look so thorough he was certain she was examining his very soul.

"Pardon my attempt at gratitude for a kind gesture. I will work on the accounts at a more convenient time."

Clara shut the book and rose to leave, her chair scraping against the floorboards. She walked across the cabin, her stride losing more of the debutante each day as her comfort grew with the sway of the airship. He stood and cut her off before she reached the door.

"Wait." He put a hand on her arm to stop her. He was at a loss of what to say, but he knew he'd never hear the end of it if Trick or Nessa saw that he had angered her. They were standing too close. She glanced at his hand quickly, then up to meet his eyes.

"Please, forgive me," he said. The request hung in the air as the moment lingered.

Then the door opened and Nessa walked in.

"I see you two are getting along better," she smirked, leaning against the door jamb. The blood warmed Clara's cheeks, and the Captain swore under his breath as he quickly released her. He turned back to the table with the maps.

"We'll hold the officer's meeting now. Clara, you may

do the books later," he said, trying to sound authoritative. He was actually glad of the interruption, despite being caught mid-apology. He needed time to think. Right now he wanted nothing more than to throw himself into planning this raid. A perfectly excusable distraction. The problem of Clara could wait.

Trick stepped in as Clara walked out. The Captain saw him glance towards the desk in the corner, then raise an eyebrow at Nessa, who gave a tiny shake of her head and a look that said it might be best not to raise the issue. The Captain decided not to comment on their conspiracy just yet. There were more important things to take care of first.

"Well. What's the latest news?"

Trick settled into his seat across the table before replying, "The latest from Robbie says there's not many who will cross our paths until next month, but there's one bringing grains to London in five days' time and we can meet it on our way to the Haven. The winds are favouring us. It's reported to be quite the haul, but we don't have as much information on the cargo as I'd like."

"Good, we'll take this opportunity. Robbie didn't express any concerns?"

"None, but I would rather learn more before we intercept the goods. We could wait until next month when Robbie and the rest of the crew are back."

"Nessa?"

"We have enough pilots to pull it off if we're careful. I don't want us taking unnecessary risks without the full crew, but the merchants up north will need these goods sooner rather than later."

"Then we'll just have to be clever about it."

"If you're certain, then I'll agree with the two of you," Trick sighed. "We'll do this raid then head north for a delivery run and pick up Robbie on the way."

"Good. Now let's be clever."

The three spoke long into the dinner hour, eating from plates brought up from the mess by Mouse. By the evening hour the plan was in place. They set course for the interception point and began preparations.

Chapter 8: In which our heroine begins to understand her choice

Clara stared down at the activity below. She was sitting aloft on the lookout platform suspended between the balloons and the foredeck with Cat and Mouse, enjoying a small snack as they took their break from training on the ropes. She had grown more and more comfortable with the heights as her training progressed. She remembered her first flight with Cat as though it were yesterday. It was so very different than gliding with her brother around the Isle. So much farther above the ground! Mouse taught her the different ways to launch oneself from the airship safely and the steps to take in an emergency. The young boy was so knowledgeable, and yet he shared the information in such an easygoing way that it was a joy to learn from him. With Cat's light frame strapped next to hers she learned to manipulate the glider along the air currents, to feel the pressure on the wings as though they were an extension of her own body. Finally, they deemed her ready to fly on her own.

It was hard to describe such a perfect experience, but Clara turned it over and over in her mind, not wanting to forget a single detail. At their signal, she allowed herself to fall forward from the ropes, giving in to the terrifying sensation of plunging toward the sea before the currents caught the wings of her glider and she steered smoothly over the water, angling around the ship. She flew in wide, sweeping arcs, feeling the rush as she climbed higher and banked her wings against the winds. She circled the balloons and dove down beneath the airship before gliding up the other side. Her body was taut and controlled, focused on every minute adjustment needed to control the glider; but her heart was open, embracing the joy and exhilaration of the flight. How could she possibly explain it? It was unlike anything she had felt before. Clara now understood why her brother was so fascinated with his inventions. He was always fiddling with his gadgets, taking things apart and putting them together again. He loved his gliders more than anything. It was one thing to go along for the ride. Flying solo was a completely different experience.

"You're thinking about it, right?" Cat asked.

"Hm?" Clara asked as she broke from her reverie.

"Your first flight! I can see that dreamy look in your eyes."

Clara reached out and tousled her curly mop of hair. Cat and her brother both had caramel-coloured curls that turned gold at the sun-kissed ends. They could have been twins but for their ages. Identical pairs of dark blue eyes shimmered with mirth. They made her miss her own brother.

"What was yours like?" she asked the younger girl.

"I've been on airships as long as I remember. Papa taught me to use a parachute when I was 4 in case there was an emergency and he couldn't reach me in time. I was flying my own glider by the time I was 7. Papa took us around in a sling when we were babes so I already knew the basics. He said Mama watches over us, so we're safe as angels."

"How old were you when...?"

Cat scrunched her nose. "When he died? Nine. Mouse was only three. He couldn't fly yet, but I found the Captain like Papa told me and we taught him."

"You must have been very brave. My father died this past spring, and I miss him very much."

"Yes," Cat said, patting Clara's hand gently. "But the Captain takes care of us now. That's what Papa said, find the Captain Duke and he will do right by you. Now we're pilots, just like him, and he's an angel with Mama."

Mouse left the wind monitors and came to sit on her other side.

"I remember him. He had a big hat. He found me in the pantry and said I must be a wee mouse because I was always getting into the food."

Clara laughed, "Is that how you came by your name?"

"Well, my real name is Morris, I suppose," he said. "But I'm really just Mouse."

"I'm Catherine! Catherine Mary Margaret Waugh."

"Well, I'm Morris Alexander James Waugh," he said. Then he leaned in to whisper in Clara's ear. "But please just call me Mouse. I like it better."

"I think Morris is a lovely name," she teased. "But you will always be Mouse to me." The young boy allowed himself to be pulled into her lap for a hug.

"Did you have no other family?"

"Some cousins, but most of them moved across the ocean. Is that where yours went, Clara?" asked Cat.

"My brother is in Oxford and my mother is in Europe visiting my aunt."

"Oh, so you'll see them again soon."

Clara sighed. She wished she could be certain, but she had a feeling it might be a long while before their paths crossed again.

"What's your name, Clara?" asked Mouse, turning his head to look up at her.

"Clara Elizabeth –" she cut herself off, noticing the Captain Duke standing below them. When he realized he had their attention, he called for them to join him and they quickly made their way down the rope ladders.

The two young pilots made it to the deck first, as usual, and were already frowning when she joined them.

"We'll be announcing the next raid at supper this evening," said the Captain.

"Well, if Clara gets to be part of it, then we do too," Cat said, crossing her arms.

"Two more years, little Cat. Not until you are –"

"Sixteen and can best Nessa in a duel. Yes, yes, we know," she said.

"In any case, Clara will be joining the two of you. I expect the two of you to show her how to take the necessary precautions."

"I know it's my first raid, but certainly I can be of some assistance," Clara interrupted. She was not pleased by the way he addressed Cat while she stood right there beside her.

"We need fighters. Experienced pilots."

Clara raised an eyebrow, "And what shall we do in the meantime? Embroidery?"

"It's not the worst idea…" the Captain began. He stopped after receiving twin glares from Clara and Cat. "Your role is to observe and learn. If you can manage that, I'll have Nessa include you in their training."

Cat and Mouse accepted their assignment and the Captain dismissed them. Then he turned to Clara.

"The raid is in three days. There's a small town we will be passing over before then. If you like, you may disembark at their port."

Clara burned.

"You wish me gone."

"I wish to know if you are committed to our cause."

"And observing this raid is to be a test of that?"

"Well, yes."

Clara sighed. "Have I not been charged with updating your account books?"

"Yes…" the Captain said, raising a quizzical brow.

"So then could it not be argued that I am already rather knowledgeable about 'our cause' and can be trusted to conduct myself in an appropriate manner? I've seen the ledgers. You target the grain shipments and other essential goods. A fifth is accounted for in trading for our own needs and payment to the crew. The rest disappears from the books." Clara paused at the Captain's stern look, taking a breath before continuing. "I am not a chartered accountant, but I have employed the double-entry system as consistently as I am able to and these missing goods must have been

transferred elsewhere. Am I correct in assuming they made it into deserving hands?"

"We can discuss this after the raid."

"Why?"

"Because our methods of obtaining these goods may not suit your sensibilities. You will observe before you make your choice."

"I have already made it through one of your raids. I saved all of you. I am quite capable of handling myself in distressing circumstances. I know I am."

"No. You know nothing. You were safely hidden away as you shall be for the next," he said, stepping in closer until she had to crane her neck to meet his gaze.

"How am I to know what it is like if I am hidden away once more?"

"Have you ever been faced with the barrel of another's gun? By the tip of their sword?"

"Well, Nessa –"

"Nessa was not trying to kill or maim you," he said. Clara raised a single brow in response. A slight smirk passed over his lips and he softened, "Clara, I cannot allow you to take part in the action until I am assured that you are battle-ready. We avoid bloodshed when we can, but we are not always successful. We fight. We steal. We kill, and are likely to do so again. We have lost pilots, good ones. You may cloak our cause as justice but never delude yourself into believing it is not crime. When you commit to this, I expect you to commit wholly, without reservation. Observe this raid before you make your choice."

Clara was silent, turning his words over in her mind. She took a deep, shaky breath and gave a curt nod. The Captain Duke reached out and drew her arms forward. He took hold of her hands, uncurling the fists they had formed at her sides.

"I am grateful to you for saving our crew. You are one of the most promising pilots I have seen in years and you fly as though you are born to it. But these are not the hands of a warrior."

Clara looked down at her hands. Soft and delicate, fingers stained black with ink. It felt strange to see them in the Captain's grasp. His own were rough from rope and wind, but they were still the hands of an artist. She shocked herself with the desire to trace the lines etched across his palm. Resisting the urge, she pulled away.

"Very well. I will stay with Cat and Mouse," she replied. Then she looked him in his eyes, "But then you will teach me to defend my crew."

He smiled, showing his teeth and dimples, "We have a deal."

The Captain left to take his turn at the watch. Clara stood tall at the rail and looked out at the horizon, deep in thought. Was this what she wanted? A life of crime? A life where she must fight, possibly even kill another? Her heart fell at the thought of losing any of the crew she had come to know and love. The Captain Duke spoke the truth. She was not prepared, not nearly. What if she was not capable after all? She would be forced to leave the airship in shame.

Clara knew the Captain would never permit her to stay unless she was a full partner to their cause. She could not endanger the rest of the crew. All her training in life was useless to her in this. She carefully considered her options. Was she really ready to commit to this life? It was time for her to acknowledge the seriousness of this venture, and Clara had never felt so unsure of herself.

Chapter 9: In which our hero learns to expect the unexpected

It was the day of the raid. The Captain Duke was making his rounds to ensure that the final preparations were underway. There was a sense of electricity in the air as the crew set themselves to their tasks with greater determination. Some had talismans hanging from their belts to bring good fortune. Others kept a lucky knot around the wrist of their shooting arm. Nessa had added small braids to the sides of her usual plait, a nod to the traditions of her ancestors.

They had disguised the airship with 'new' scrollwork and canvas to avoid detection. Today they were the *QueenSparrow*. It was one of Cat's and Mouse's favourite games, thinking of new names for the airship. The hull had seen many monikers in its time, and worn several guises in its travels. The Captain Duke had his own secret name for his airship, a name only he and Trick knew from the midnight christening after her liberation from a Tradist dock. Names had power, and he was more aware of their potency than most.

She was a beautiful ship with solid, lightweight decks and sturdy lines. Her balloons were replaced each season and the double lining held multiple individual chambers to decrease the risk of an explosion. The Captain had studied the dynamics of different airships for years before choosing his, and he made sure to look into every innovation. An explosion almost a decade ago on a passenger ship had inspired a great deal of technological advances and improvements to the safety of modern airships. It was a different story, however, when you meant to stay in the air regardless of who was trying to shoot you down.

They were drifting over the forested countryside, waiting for the other ship to come into sight. He heard Cat shout down to her brother. Mouse conveyed the message from his position halfway down the ropes:

"Airship sighted off the starboard bow! It's coming from the west!"

The two youths scrambled to descend the ladders. Cat gave the precise location of the other ship and the Captain Duke sent a message to the navigator to adjust their position accordingly. The gliders were on standby, and the rudder was partially disabled. They were able to manoeuver by adjusting the angle of the propellers, but for the plan to work they needed to seem stuck.

"Cat, take Mouse and Clara and stay down in the cabins. You know what to do."

"Yes Captain," she said.

He exchanged a look with Clara as she came to join them. The Captain's resolve wavered, but it was too late to turn course with the other ship so near. Cat and Mouse were born to this life, but stowaway or no, he had his doubts about Clara. If all was above board there would be little trouble today. Still, the risk to her safety would have to be endured.

"Stay below and keep out of trouble."

Clara's sigh was echoed with identical eye rolls from Cat and Mouse.

"Come now Clara, the dear Captain Duke has entrusted me with your well-being. You must teach us this embroidery you speak of," Cat sang as she ushered her little brother to the stairs, linking with Clara's arm as she went. He watched until they were safely below, and returned to the preparations.

The other airship was a heavier model with three huge balloons taking on its weight. Its cargo was concealed in a large hold. The Captain smiled at the size of it; there must be a great deal on board to merit the lift required to carry it. He stood and watched it grow as it neared until he could read the writing on its side: The *Highflyer*. Its midship deck bustled with activity as the crew gathered to get a look at him. He had only a few of his pilots with him, the cooks, a few medics, and Trick. When they were close enough, he raised his hand to hail the other captain.

"In the name of the Queen, your assistance, please!"

"What is the nature of your inquiry?" the other captain called back. The '*QueenSparrow*' had raised its flag indicating distress.

"Our rudder has unfortunately fallen into disrepair. Would you have any spare parts to assist us?"

The other captain turned to confer with his lieutenants. From the corner of his eye, the Captain Duke caught sight of a shadow passing over the other ship's balloons. He smiled to himself. The gliders were in place. It was all according to plan. He kept his sight on his counterpart, who finished discussing the matter with the crew and turned back with his reply.

"Our apologies, but we are unable to be of assistance at this time. We have an urgent delivery that is expected on the coast. We'll send word by telegraph to the nearest port to assist you as soon as they are able."

"I'm afraid that is unacceptable," he replied. The Captain Duke savoured the look of confusion that crossed their faces as he signaled his crew.

Chaos reigned as twelve gliders landed smoothly on the opposite side of the *Highflyer*'s decks, each with an extra pilot strapped in front who quickly released themselves, ready for battle. They protected their partner as the gliders' wings were drawn in, providing the perfect distraction as the Captain Duke and his crew took up an offensive position in seconds. Nessa was an intimidating figure at the centre of the glider crew, both pistols raised and ready. The others had short swords held before them, better for close fighting. The *Highflyer* was immediately compromised. The other captain turned back angrily.

"You will regret this, pirate!"

"Surrender your ship and we will only take what we need. No harm will come to you or your crew. You have my word."

"Oh, you can be certain there will be harm today!" the other man shouted as his face turned a disturbing shade of red. The Captain Duke smiled with a dare in his eyes as adrenalin flooded his veins in preparation for the fight. A witty retort was on his lips when he saw the door of the other ship's hold open with a glint of steel.

Dozens of soldiers streamed out onto the decks, taking a defensive position quickly and turning on his crew members. Seven gliders were able to get off amid the chaos, some grabbing their partners by the harness with no time to strap them in properly. Nessa sent her own glider off without her as she fought to give the others time to escape. The Captain watched in horror, jumping onto the rail and holding the lines for balance as he raised his gun.

"No!" he thundered. "Stop this at once!"

He saw at least three soldiers nursing bullet wounds from Nessa's pistols, but there was no way to get to his crew members with the odds against them. He felt helpless as he caught her eye and saw her look of surrender. She aimed upwards at one of the *Highflyer*'s balloons to fire but was tackled by four soldiers before she could make the shot. The rest of the glider crew was subdued while Nessa was dragged across the deck, fighting her captors all the way. She got in a few good kicks before they made it to the captain. He aimed a pistol at her temple as they forced her head up to look at him.

"Stop. Let us parlay."

The other man grinned. He pulled his arm back and struck Nessa across her skull. The Captain Duke reeled at the sight as his bravest fighter crumpled to the floor. A hand grasped his coat and he glanced down to see Trick restraining him with a look of warning. The soldiers were lined along the *Highflyer*'s deck, some aiming at himself, others for their balloon. His own crew was lined up with guns at the ready, waiting on his word. They had little hope of escaping the situation; retaliation was out of the question with Nessa incapacitated on board. Not unless he was willing to sacrifice his own pilots.

"Well, pirate?" the other captain called over with an evil look, "Are you prepared to surrender?"

The Captain Duke was running out of options. Perhaps he could still save his crew if he went along with them, but more than likely they'd be jailed under the worst conditions with no reputation to warrant better treatment. The Captain Duke was ready to take drastic measures when he caught movement from the corner of his eye.

The door to his own crew's quarters opened. The Captain Duke yelled a warning to take cover, but choked on his words as he struggled to conceal his shock. Clara the Pilot was gone. Before him, Clara the Debutante stepped into the sun dressed in an afternoon gown, shading her eyes with a parasol as Cat followed behind. She smiled demurely at him, then turned as though noticing the other airship for the first time, and screamed.

Chapter 10: In which our heroine takes matters into her own hands

Clara felt the blood rush to her head as she stared at the full complement of soldiers with their guns aimed at the airship. She had watched the tables turn through the window with Cat and Mouse. Panicked, she tried to go above to help, but the children blocked her path. They needed some kind of diversion to buy more time. She berated herself for only knowing silly rules of etiquette instead of swordplay. She was useless here. Then, the idea had caught her and she set the two youths to work as she pinned her hair quickly and gathered her weapons. The wardrobe held everything they needed to make the ruse work. Fortunately, the street clothes were designed for easy wearing. She set Cat's hair as best as she could, racing through the instructions as Mouse helped to lace them both into gowns.

Clara took a deep breath before opening the door, silently thanking the owner of the dress she wore for having a generous waistline so she was less likely to faint from lack of air. Facing the soldiers, however, she thought she might risk fainting after all. She caught the Captain Duke's look of astonishment before shrieking at the sight of the *Highflyer*. She rushed to him with a dramatic sweep of her parasol before dropping it to grasp the tail of his coat.

"Oh, Captain! What is the meaning of this?"

She wasn't sure who looked more shocked: the Captain Duke, the crew, or the soldiers. The Captain gave a wary glance to the guns pointed at them, then jumped down to stand on the deck with her. She buried herself in his arms.

"Please, my lady, calm yourself," he said loudly, then held her close and whispered, "*What* are you doing?"

"Play along. Trust me," she whispered back. She clung to his arm, feeling the muscles tensed beneath the fabric. Any amusement she might have in his discomfort vanished at the sight of Nessa's limp form.

"Nessa!" she cried, with real concern. She grasped the rail and stared down the other captain, collecting herself to play her role. She had to get this right, for all their sakes.

"What have you done to her? I am Lady Margaret Winstead. My father is an advisor to Her Royal Highness Princess Beatrice! You will have your men stand down at once and return our dear officer to us."

The soldiers began to look doubtful. The captain glared back but a sergeant stepped in to whisper in his ear.

"Does the British Crown know of this? I will take this matter directly to Her Majesty the Queen!" she continued. "Command your men to stand down and return our crew members." She turned to glance at Cat, who hurried over.

"Margaret! We must return below. They have to be pirates, we are lost!" The young girl clung to her side with a look of terror.

Now the soldiers began to lower their weapons. The sergeant gave a sharp reprimand to the *Highflyer*'s captain and stepped in front of him. Clara watched them from the corner of her eye as she consoled Cat.

"Heavens, do not tremble so dear sister, it is only a misunderstanding of some sort." Cat was silently shaking with laughter, hiding her face in Clara's shoulder. Clara directed Cat, doing her best impression of a frightened girl, to the arms of Trick to explain the plan. She looked up to the Captain. It was time for him to play his part. She only hoped that he guessed her intentions correctly as he shielded her from the guns on the other deck.

"My lady, I told you to remain below, it is not safe."

She swooned gracefully, clutching at his arms as he held her up.

"My dear Captain, I just could not hide in that stuffy cabin any longer, not with you brave souls risking your lives. I just had to see what the matter was."

He stared down the other men and shouted,

"Sir, I am not prepared to surrender my ship with such valuable cargo aboard. We are in need of assistance. I apologize for the ruse, but as I'm sure you know there are pirates in these parts and we thought it best to take the offense to scare potential attackers away."

The flustered captain sputtered his objection as the sergeant signaled his men to lower their arms.

"You would have me believe that you were not trying to attack this ship? You are pirates! The whole lot of you!"

"Pirates?" Clara laughed delicately, "I should hope not. The dear Captain is an old family friend. We have chartered his ship to take us to a village in East Anglia that's seen terrible drought this year. We are taking some of our own small store of grain to assist the farmers. Our governess has family in the area and we thought it a fitting tribute as she— as she— Ohhh!" Clara turned into the Captain Duke's arms and began to weep piteously. Cat let out her own terrifying wail and buried her face in her hands. Clara took a peek and could see that Cat was shaking with silent laughter as Trick patted her shoulder awkwardly. The Captain Duke handed her a handkerchief, and she dabbed at her own dry eyes.

"I am so sorry, I don't mean to cause a scene. It was just such a tremendous loss. My sister and I feel it terribly."

The sergeant stepped forward and removed his hat. The rest of the soldiers followed suit as the *Highflyer*'s captain grew redder and madder. The sergeant gave him a look of censure and called out:

"My deepest apologies, Miss Winstead, we truly meant no offense. One cannot be too careful in these parts. Please forgive our colleague's indiscretion. Captain, I believe you initially hailed for assistance. What do you require?"

"My thanks, sir. Do you have a spare blade aboard? Your captain did not think it fit to give aid."

The sergeant conferred with the first mate as the captain continued to sputter his objections and then called over, "We do, in fact. My men and I will bring it over. May a small party have permission to board? Your crew is free to go."

The Captain Duke nodded, "Yes, please be welcome. You have our greatest thanks for your charity and understanding." He directed the crew to extend a platform between the two ships.

Trick crossed first to help bring Nessa safely over. Cat

hurried off with the medics to attend to her below deck. Three men and the first mate joined the sergeant to assist with the installation of the new piece.

"My apologies for the injury to your pilot, but I believe she will recover fully. In fairness, she did nearly take out a number of my own men," the sergeant said as he joined them. He introduced himself as the leader of his contingent.

"We were both acting in our own defense, sir. Welcome aboard the *QueenSparrow*. I am Captain Edward Manning."

Clara did her best to ease the lingering tension between the two men. She played her role as the Lady Winstead, walking elegantly about the ship with the Captain Duke on one arm and the sergeant on the other as she chattered on about how refreshing it was to journey by the air, and elaborating on the mission for the grain.

"We have just over a score of sacks for seeding, but we do hope to locate more. This was as much as our estate could spare at the moment, but it is our Christian duty to see to others' care as well as our own. And Miss Ellington is the perfect image of charity and kindness. That is, she was——." She stopped to gaze over the landscape below, looking so heartbroken and forlorn that the Captain seemed caught by the play himself, pressing his hand over her own in comfort. Thankfully, the sergeant felt the hook too.

"My dear lady, I feel for your loss. I am sure we could spare some of our own stock to add to your mission."

Clara brightened, and could see the sergeant was completely lost.

"Oh would you? Oh that would be most welcome, thank you dear sergeant!" She clasped his hand and blushed.

"Forgive me; it is rather splendid to know such good men are taking care of our skies. Are you certain it will be no trouble for you?"

"Not at all. A percentage is always assumed as spoilage in their calculations. It will not be missed. We have a rather large cargo this journey, my men and I were sent to ensure its safety." The sergeant puffed his chest with pride. Clara sensed the Captain stiffen beside her.

"Thank you, it is most kind of you. Our dear Miss Ellington would be so honoured by your generosity."

The Captain Duke thanked the sergeant graciously as well, and sent some of his own crew to help carry over another four dozen sacks over the other captain's objections. Clara chatted on about the Season and country life and insisted that the sergeant call on her family in London at any time. Finally, repaired and restocked, the ships parted ways, as Clara waved the handkerchief gracefully in farewell until the *Highflyer* faded into the horizon.

When they could no longer see the other ship, she collapsed, laughing, on the deck. When her amusement subsided, she looked up to see the Captain standing above her with arms crossed.

"Oh don't look so sour. It worked, did it not?"

"Lady Winstead, if I recall, is a dour blonde at least 10 years your senior."

"Yes, and a dreadful bore as well."

"And what will her family think when an unfamiliar sergeant comes to their door, praising their daughter for her

81

charity and offering condolences for the loss of their dear governess?"

"I imagine they'll wish the fiction was true."

The Captain shook his head, not bothering to conceal his smile, and helped her up to stand with him.

"I'll admit it. You have saved us all for a second time. That was clever, getting the grain from him despite it all."

"How far was I from the truth?"

She saw him hesitate, grappling with the decision to trust her or not. Finally, he sighed, "We're going up the western coast, not the east. But yes, we'll be delivering it to those in need."

He turned away to stare at the landscape before them, "I nearly had a heart attack when I saw the two of you all dressed up."

"It was a near thing. It was lucky there were some that fit well enough. It would have been harder to explain a dusty ball gown if I'd had to use my own."

"We'll have to find better ones if we pull it off again."

"I don't think I like playing the simpering maiden. Did you see their inspection logs? I caught a look when the first mate had them brought over to calculate how much they could spare. We could play that angle instead."

"What do you mean?"

"Fly under the inspector's flag. Come in to inspect the stores and take a few as samples to test for spoilage or something. I know enough of trade law to make it work, and I can make up a passable receipt for them as well," she explained. In fact, she had studied her father's books on trade economics extensively. The library was her favourite escape in their home, and her family excused her proclivity to read everything in sight as long as she reported dutifully to her etiquette classes as well.

The Captain Duke considered her proposal. "I'll admit we have not tried such a thing before, but the Tradist ships are under heavier guard these days." He reached out to shake her hand. "We'll make a good team."

The wind caught at her skirts, blowing the material around his legs as he steadied her. Clara blushed and excused herself to change. She could feel his eyes on her as she crossed the decks to descend to the quarters below. She checked to see that Nessa was recovering, and shared a long hug with Cat and Mouse. Her heart soared at their success. The donated grain from the *Highflyer* would help their cause a great deal. The Captain Duke trusted her now.

As she dressed herself in her pilot's clothes once again, she stared at the gown laid out on the bed.

Well, well, Clara, she thought. *It's a pilot's life for me!*

Stay tuned for Book Two!

**Tales of the Captain Duke:
From Haven to Hell**

Preview: From Haven to Hell

It was a fine, cloudless day. A terrible day to mount an attack from the skies. But the weather could not be helped, and the Captain Duke and his crew could not delay this dreaded moment any longer. Clara's knuckles were bone white as she clutched the railing of the airship. The land below was lush and green, with rolling hills bending into the distance, shrouded in the early morning mists. A ribbon of river could be glimpsed curving through the trees, feeding into a large lake nearby. She had always wanted to visit the Lake District. The area was known far and wide for its natural beauty, particularly now that the forests and rivers nestled in the valleys between the fells could be viewed in all their glory from above. She regretted only the circumstances of their visit. The airship was battle-ready, armed gliders prepared to leap at a moment's notice from the bow and stern. Soon they would reach the Haven, and the battle would begin.

The Captain Duke approached to stand beside her. Lost in her thoughts, she startled at his touch as he rested a hand on her arm and pointed to steer her gaze.

"Over there, beyond those cliffs. We're circling our approach to follow the regular shipping routes to Keswick. The Haven is on an island in the Derwentwater, we'll see it soon." He frowned, "Are you alright?"

"Just a few nerves. Tell me more about it. What is it like?"

"It's an old manor house. The only one on the isle. It's surrounded by thick forest on all sides, with a clearing cut to the north for the port and cargo loaders. I found it years ago with Trick when we were looking for a place to hide out from a storm. We fixed it up, made friends with the locals. We made it into a haven. The Haven. Our home." He sighed, "I planned its defenses myself, and now I must exploit its weaknesses."

"Is it certain that we should expect trouble? Is there any likelihood that the Haven is not compromised?"

The Captain Duke stared far into the distance, gripping the railing. "A small chance, but it is not a risk we can afford."

Clara could hardly believe it had only been a week since the raid. It had turned into a perilous standoff between the Captain Duke's pilots and a full complement of soldiers who were guarding the large shipment of grain. It was her etiquette training that saved the day. Dressed as a highborn lady, she persuaded the sergeant to believe the entire incident was a misunderstanding. She secured his favour, as well as a substantial donation of grain for the 'impoverished village of her late governess.' But despite the favourable ending, the event was not without its costs.

"There. Do you see it?" he asked, leaning forward over the rail. His posture was tense, his brow creased with worry, and yet, Clara could see his longing, his anticipation to see his home. She said nothing, but laid a hand over his as the island came into view. It was a beautiful sight, the natural elevation according it a dramatic flair as it rose above the deep blue waves.

"You should go below," he said after a moment. "Nessa will be attempting her escape."

She couldn't help the smirk that crossed her face, but was reassured by his matching smile. She squeezed his hand, "There's still hope."

His smile faded.

"Tend to Nessa. She needs your care."

Clara wished she could ease his fears. He stood before her with his hair unbound, fiery waves swept across his shoulders by the wind. She wanted to tuck one of the bright strands behind his ear and tell him everything would be alright. Instead, she gave a curt nod and descended to the cabins below.

Acknowledgements

My deepest gratitude to everyone who has supported me in pursuing this dream. Thanks to Jon Lawless for being the best cheerleader and for his CAPS LOCK enthusiasm, to Laura Sinclair for always asking for more, to Arden Dier for being my first beta reader, to Paola Loriggio for her editing prowess, and to Valorie Curry for calling me a writer before I knew I was one.

Thanks to all my family for sharing in this joy. My parents, Ray and Kelly; my sister, Leah, for all our bedtime stories; my brother, Andrew, for his excellent business sense; and extra thanks to my very talented sister, Sarah, for bringing the Captain Duke's airship to life for the cover.

This book is particularly dedicated to the memory of my maternal grandparents, who saw the beginning of this book, but not the end. Grandma was a reader, and I'm so happy she had the chance to hear this story before she passed. Grandpa taught me about strength, dedication and hard work, and told us to do what we love. Well, I am.

Thanks to the thousands of authors whose books have filled my shelves and my imagination, and a special thanks to Neil Gaiman, who told me to finish things and said that I would do just fine.

Thanks to the lovely staff at Café Pamenar, the Bean Cellar, Frog Ponds Café, and Bridgehead for the caffeine, company and encouragement.

This started as a notebook of scribbled ideas. And now, I'm finally able to bring these worlds to life. So my final thanks are to you, Reader.

I hope you enjoy these adventures as much as I do.

--Rebecca Diem
August 2014

Rebecca Diem grew up in a far-off land known as Chatsworth, Ontario, surrounded by hills and forests and streams and strange metal beasts that tore through the landscape leaving iron in their wake.

And one day she began to write it all down...

Web: http://RebeccaDiem.com
Email: rebeccadiemauthor@gmail.com
Facebook: www.facebook.com/RebeccaDiemAuthor
Twitter/Instagram: @kthnxbex

Thank you so much for supporting my work.
Please share, rate and review!